Meet Happy, Max, and Trixie

Happy

Max

Trixie

"Happy," Max said, "come on out of the truck. This is going to be a great day."

"We'll spend the day at the beach, enjoying ourselves, and we'll find lots of fun ways to play."

"We'll hunt for shells and dig in the sand, and after that, we'll have our picnic lunch, just as we planned."

So Happy, Max, and Trixie the mouse, each unpacked their beach things.

"Can we build a sand castle Max?" asked Happy, "and then pretend we are kings?"

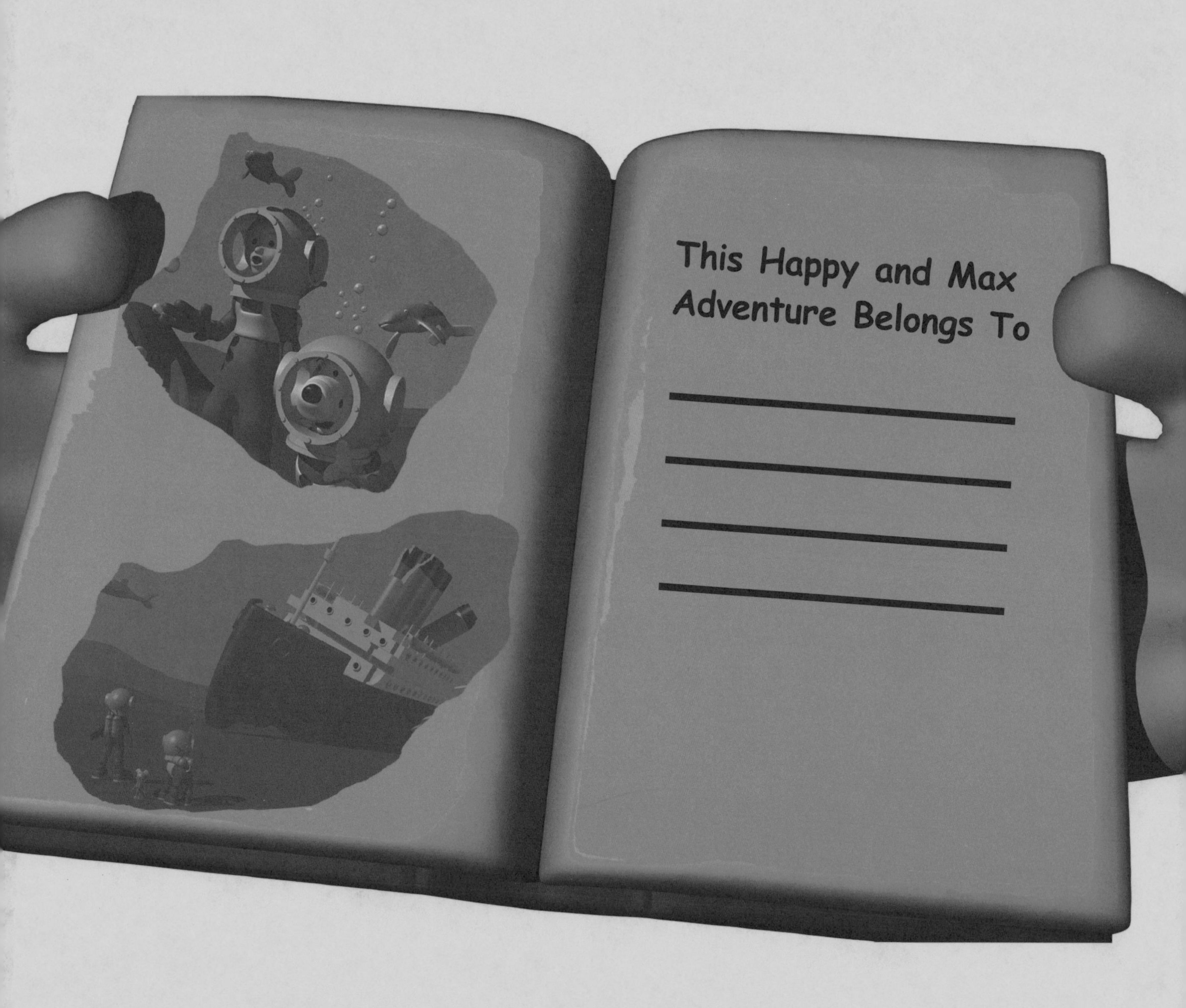
This Happy and Max
Adventure Belongs To

HAPPY and MAX
The Sunken Ship Adventure
Story by Kris Jamsa, Ph.D.
Illustrations by Art Vandeleigh

Happy and Max
The Sunken Ship Adventure

Story by Kris Jamsa, Ph.D.
Illustrations by Art Vandeleigh

...a young reader's best friend™

ISBN 1-884133-86-X

Jamsa Press
2975 South Rainbow Suite I
Las Vegas, NV 89102
www.jamsa.com

For information about translations and product licensing of books in the Kids Interactive Happy and Max series, please write to Jamsa Press, 2975 South Rainbow Suite I, Las Vegas, NV 89102.

Printed in the USA 98765432

For information on other books in the Kids Interactive Happy and Max series, visit our Web site at *www.HappyAndMax.com.*

Wearing their sunglasses and beach clothes, the three made their way.

"Let's find a perfect spot Happy," Max said, "where we can set up our things for the day."

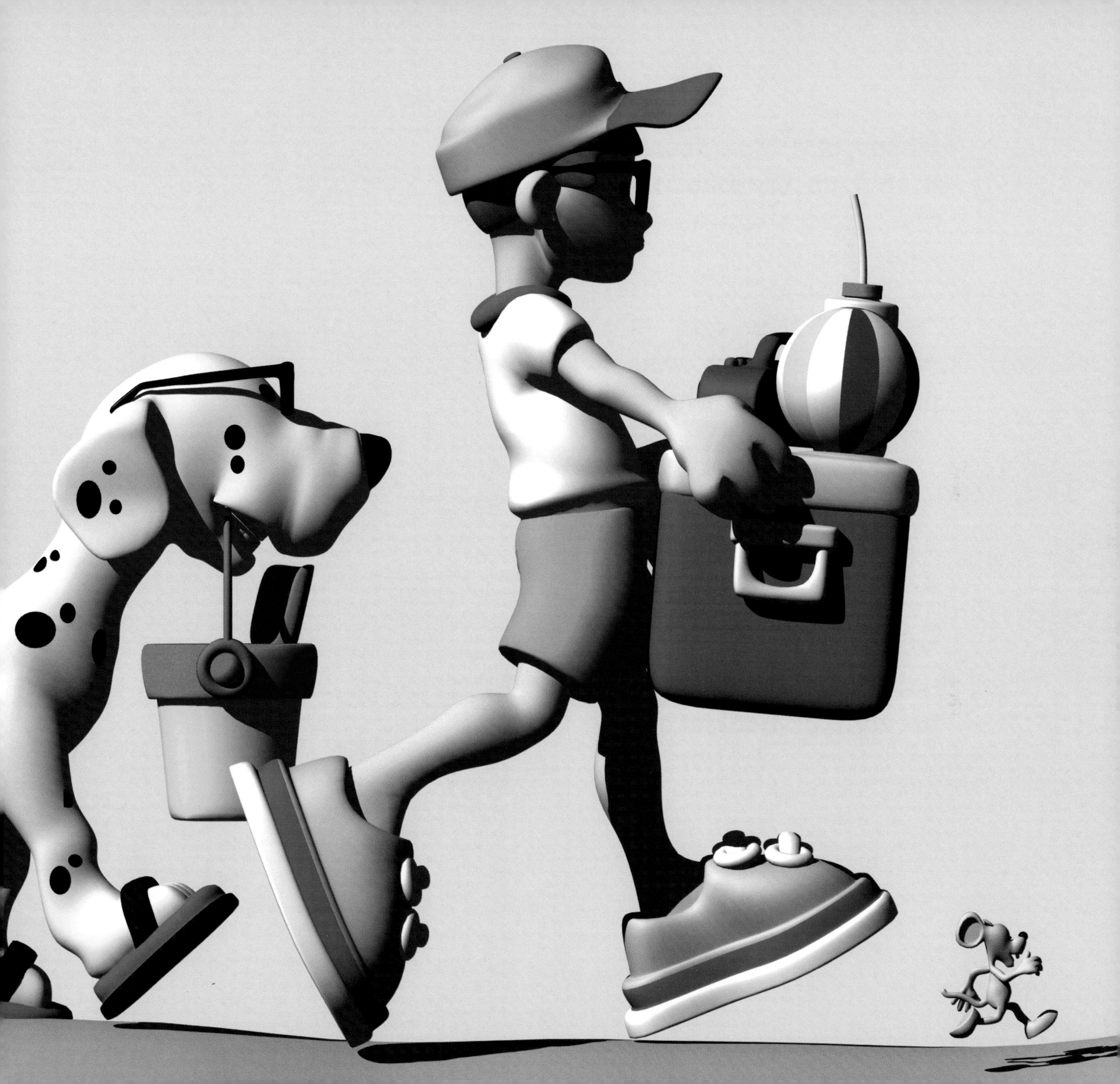

Happy and Max found
a spot on the beach,
that gave them a very
nice view.

"Happy," Max said, "let's
relax here for a while,
until we decide what
to do."

"Happy," said Max, "take
a look around. We've got
everything that we need."

"We've got sodas, toys,
and music, and I even
brought us books to read."

So Happy laid down on his blanket, and Max leaned back in his chair.

Max read a book on deep sea diving, while Happy read a story about three bears.

Soon, however, Happy
was no longer reading.

He'd fallen asleep on
his blanket, and was
now busy dreaming.

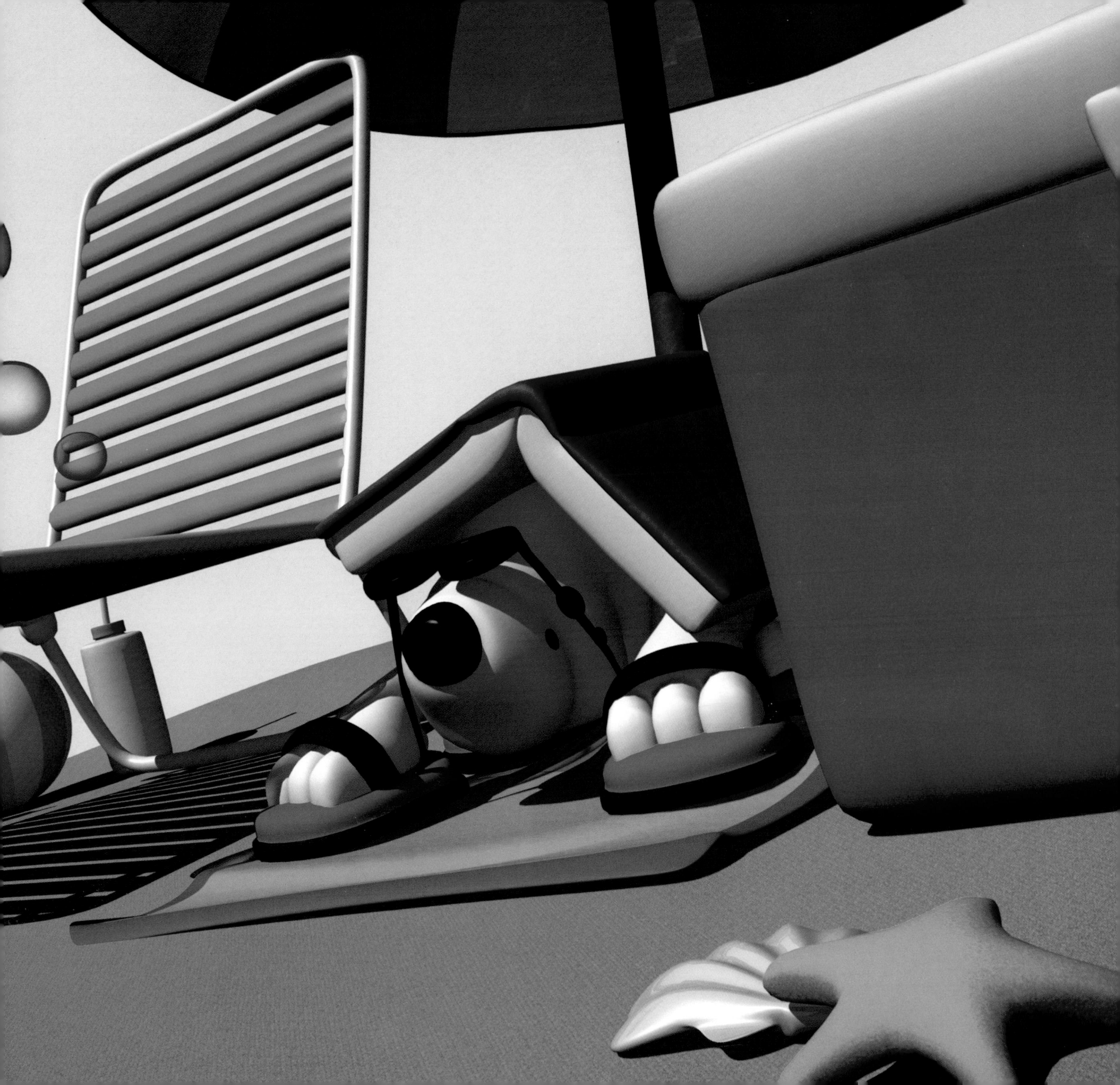

From within his deep sleep, Happy heard a noise from nearby.

But not yet wanting to wake up, Happy opened only one eye.

At first Happy couldn't see the cause of the noise that had made him stir.

Then suddenly, in front of Happy, walked a giant sea monster!

"Aggggh!" barked Happy, as he jumped back in the air.

"A sea monster!" yelled Happy, as he knocked over the chair.

"Aggggh!" Happy barked again and again, hoping that someone would hear.

As Happy barked even louder for help, the sea monster covered its ears!

Happy tried his best to act very brave, and not to show the fear he felt inside.

"Run, Happy!" shouted Trixie the mouse. "Happy, find somewhere to hide!"

Happy was too scared to run. So he chose instead, just to sit.

Then, while the monster stood in front of Happy, it began to loosen its helmet.

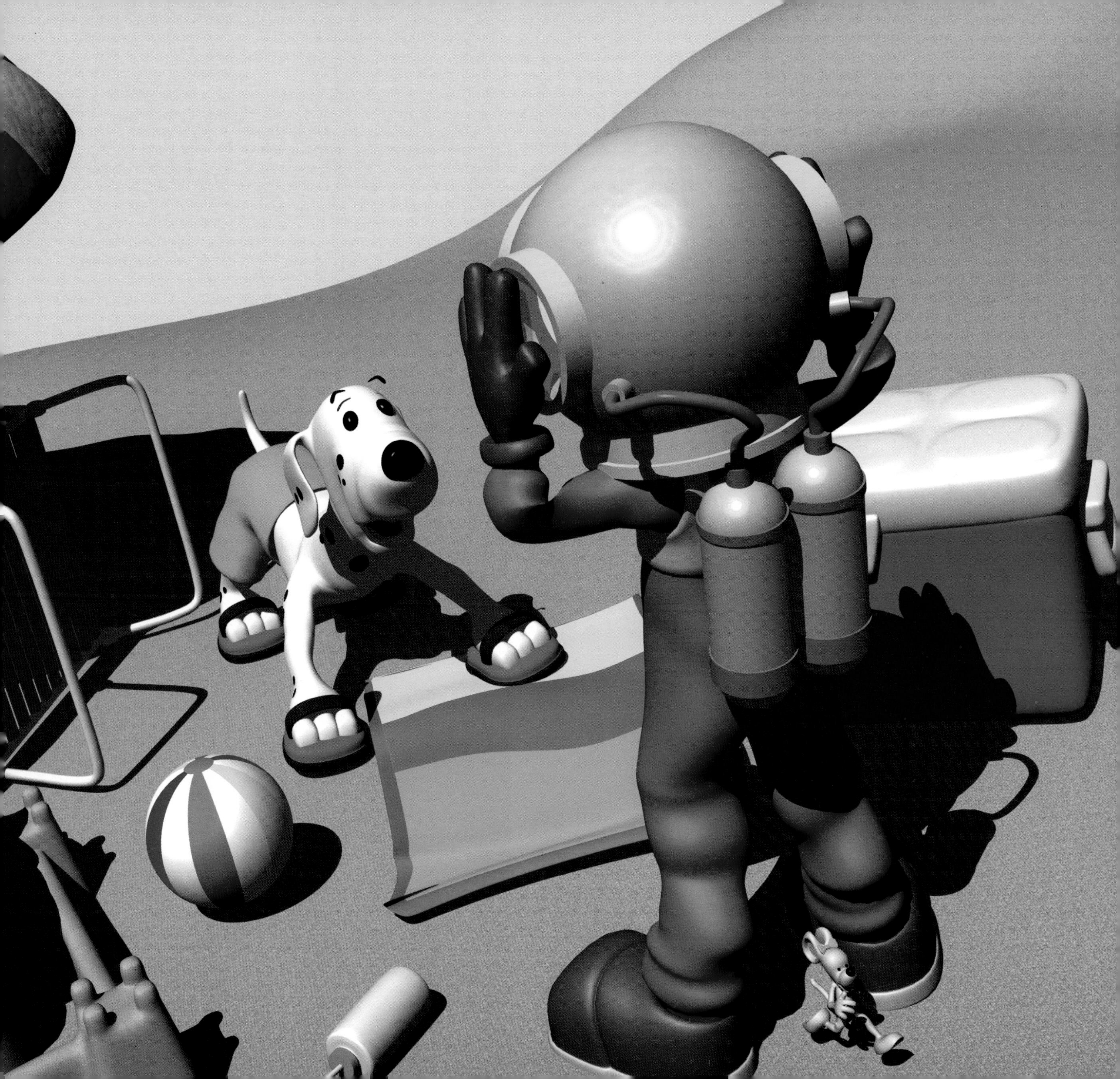

"I should have run with Trixie," Happy thought, "and found a safe place to hide."

But when the sea monster took off its helmet, Happy was surprised to find that Max was inside!

"Max! It's you!" Happy shouted.

"Why are you wearing that mask? Why are you wearing that outfit, and those shoes?" Happy nervously asked.

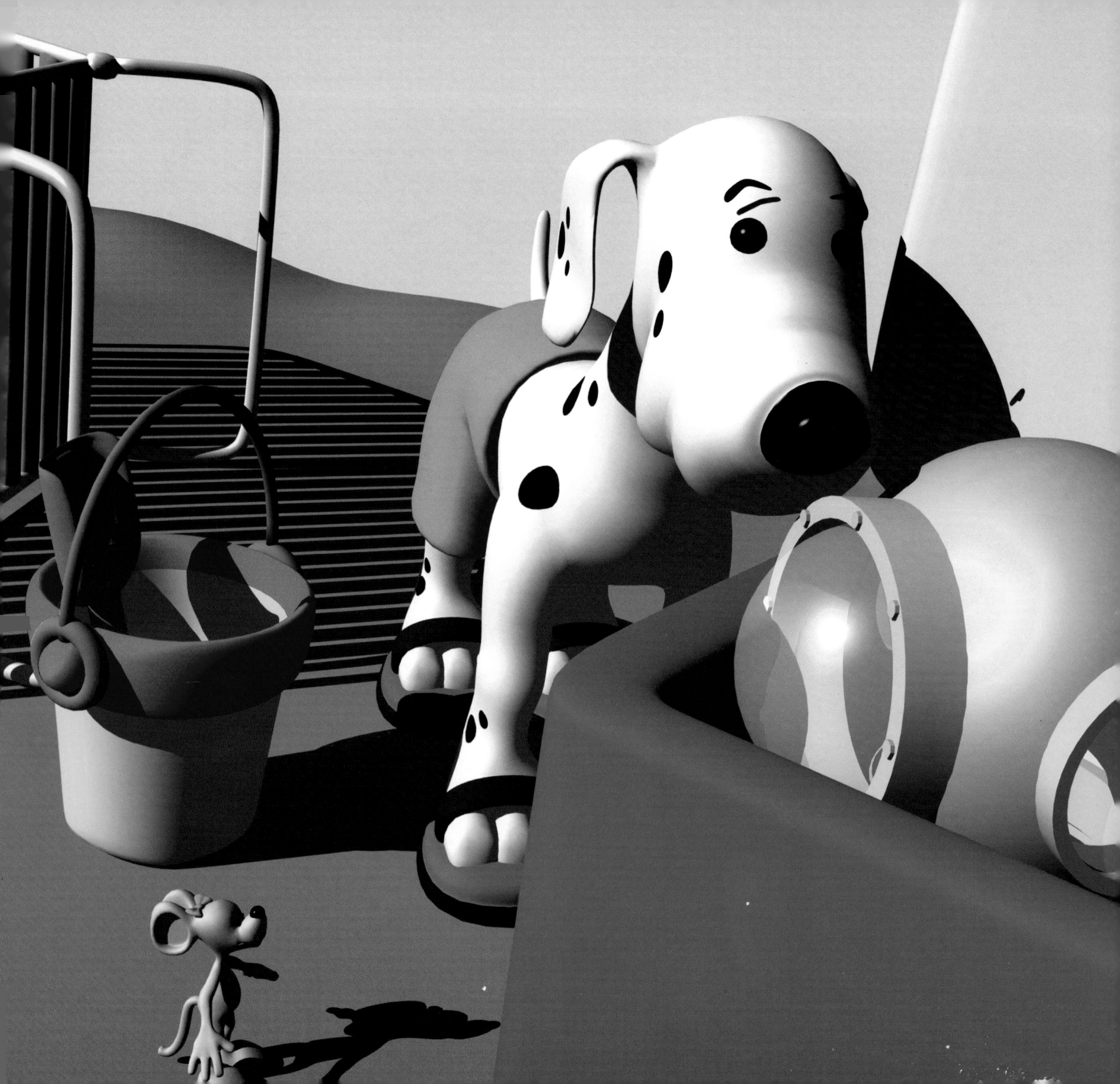

"This is a deep sea-diver's suit Happy," said Max. "I thought diving is what we should do."

"I've got this outfit for me, and I brought suits for both of you."

"By wearing these outfits, Happy," Max said, "we can explore the bottom of the sea."

"We'll encounter underwater rocks, plants, and fish. It will be fun. You'll like it. You'll see."

Happy laughed at Trixie, as they both put on their sea-diving suits.

They snickered as they fastened their helmets, and giggled as they laced up their boots.

Happy looked down at Trixie, who in turn, looked back at him.

"Let's give sea diving a try, Trixie," Happy said. "I say we should go take a swim."

Happy and Trixie caught up with Max, who was waiting for them on the shore.

"Over there, Happy," said Max, as he pointed, "that's where we'll start to explore."

Happy looked again at Trixie, and then looked back at the sea.

"A dog and a mouse underwater," Happy thought to himself, "I don't understand how this can be."

"Let's go explore the ocean!" said Max, as the three waded into the waves.

"Maybe we'll climb undersea mountains, or look inside undersea caves."

The three headed into the water, which suddenly became quite deep.

"I wish," Happy thought to himself, "I was still back on my blanket fast asleep."

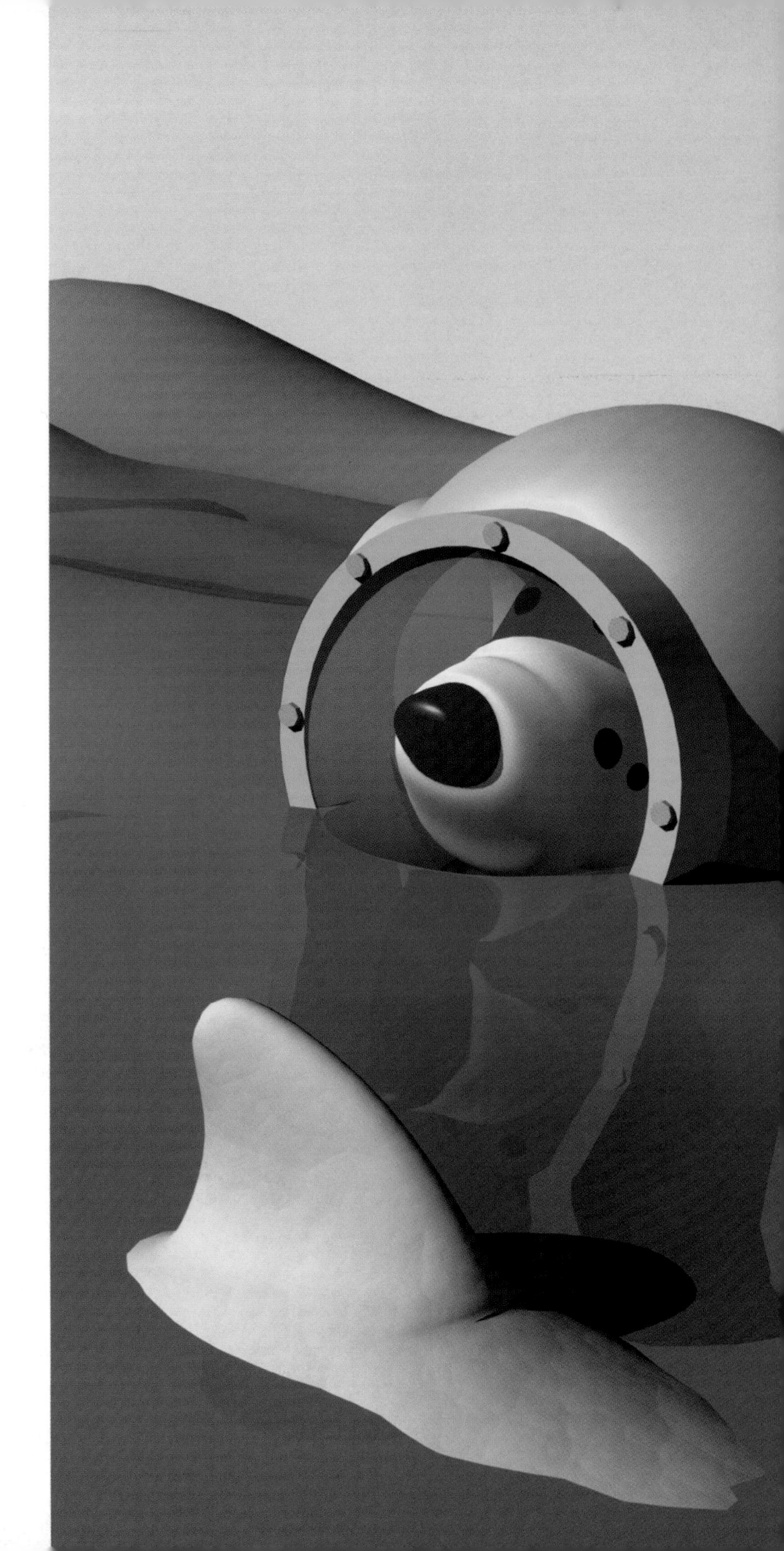

"Hey," Happy barked, as
he looked out his mask,
"this is really quite neat!"

"I can see birds flying
above in the air, and
fish swimming below past
my feet."

Happy, Max, and Trixie set off to explore the ocean floor.

They saw crabs, coral, and fish, but they still wanted to see more.

Happy and Max found a large reef, which was home to lots of sea plants.

"Look Happy," laughed Max, as he looked at the reef, "the waves make those giant plants dance!"

Happy and Max kept exploring, not quite sure what else they would see.

Suddenly, Trixie rode by on a sea horse and shouted, "Hey Happy, take a look at me!"

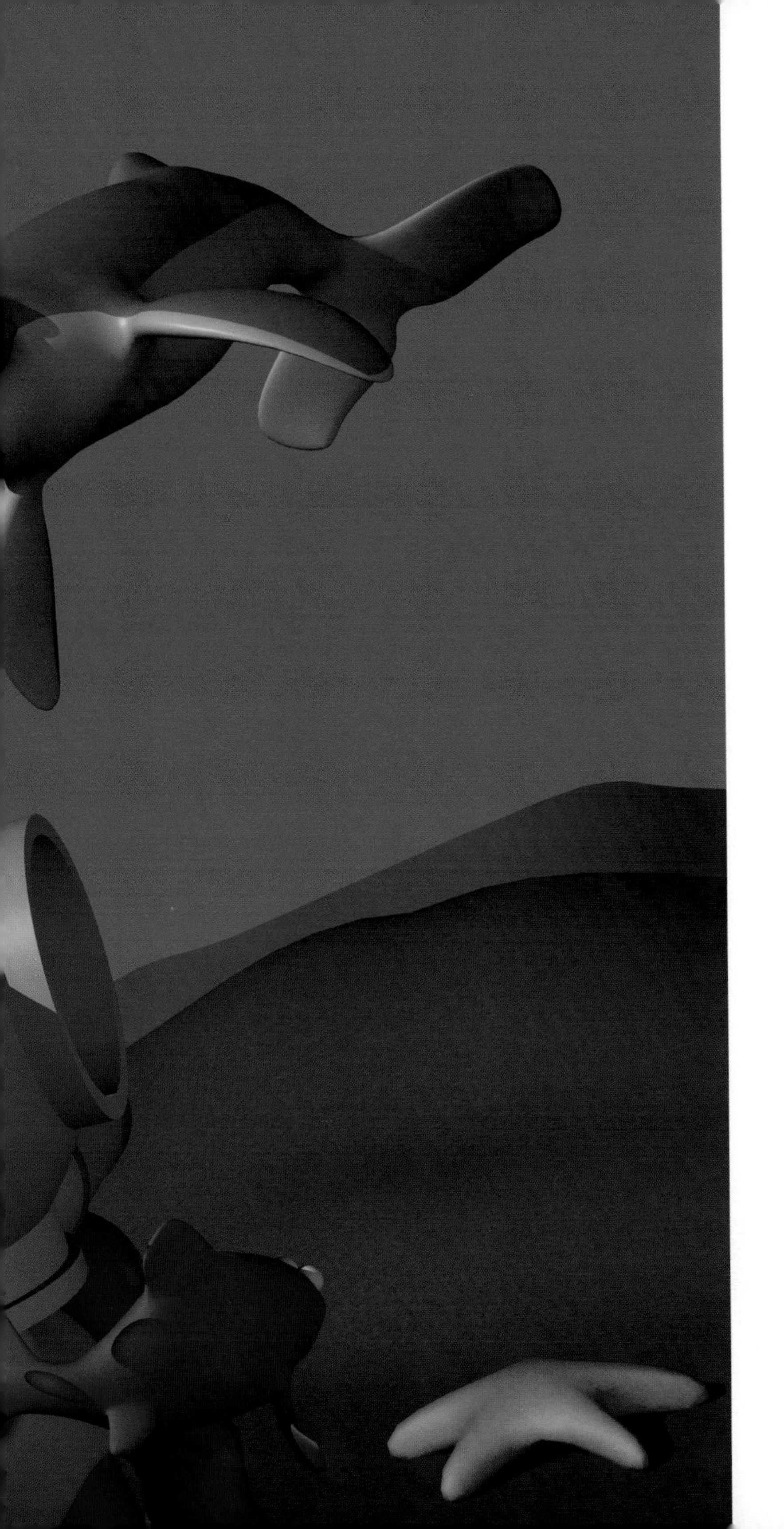

Happy and Max walked past the great reef, as they searched the vast ocean floor.

Suddenly, they both stopped right where they stood, having found something new to explore.

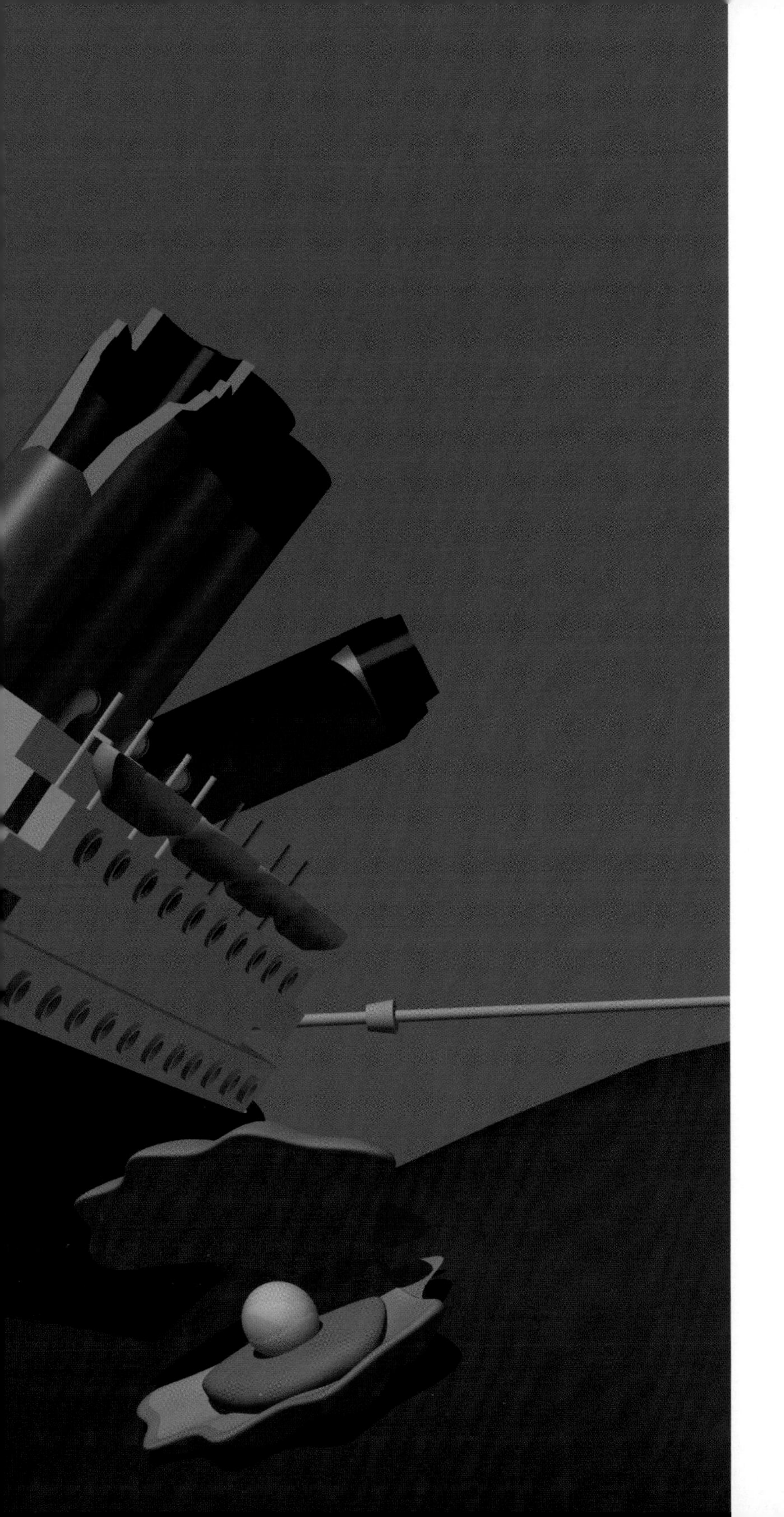

"Look at that sunken ship, Happy," Max said. "Wow! That boat is *gigantic*!"

"Max," Happy barked as he looked at the ship, "could that boat be the Titanic?"

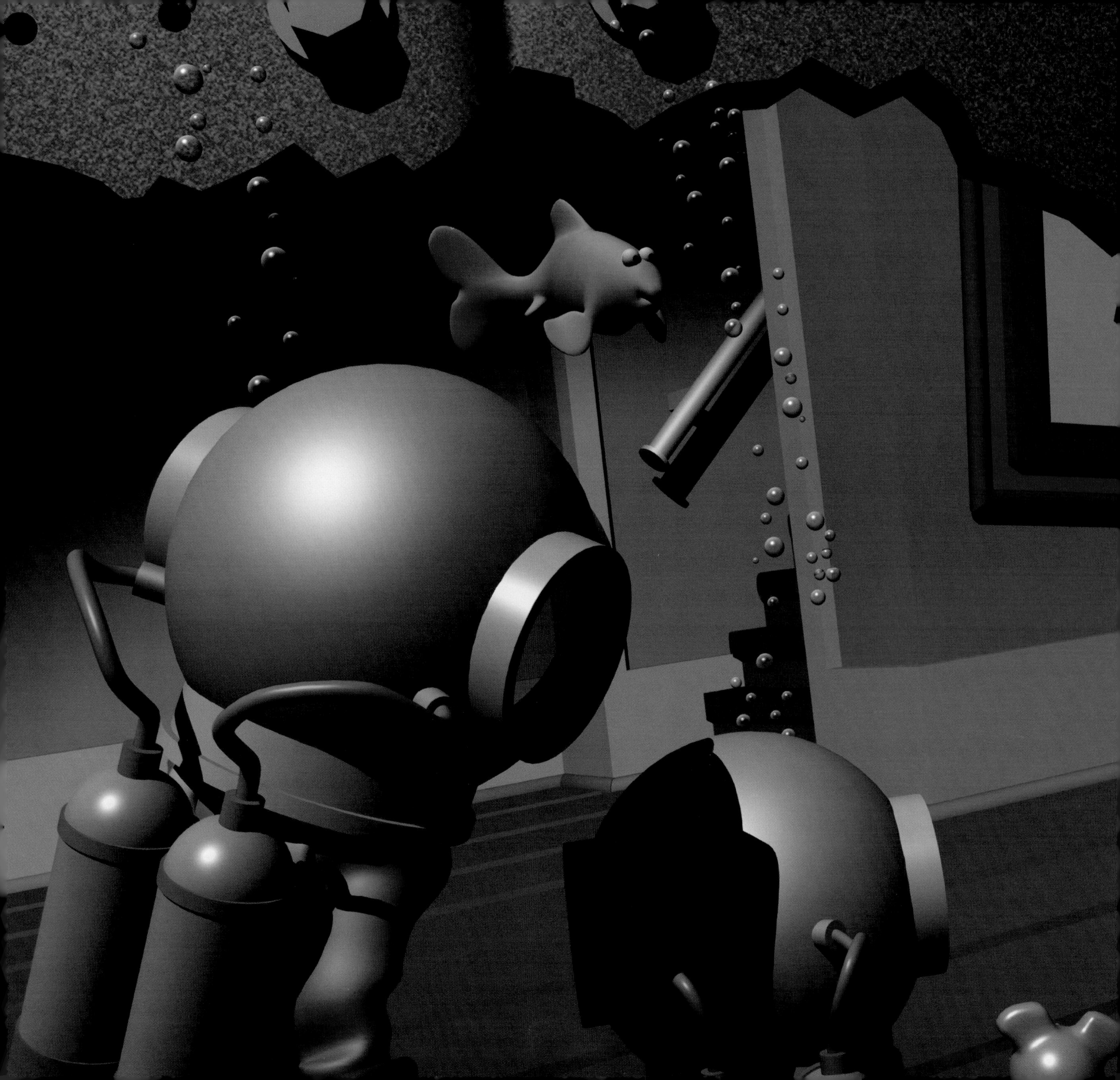

As Happy and Max made
their way around the
great ship, they found
a hole in the boat where
the metal had ripped.

"Look over there, Happy,"
Max said, "we can see
inside."

"You go ahead first, Max,"
Happy said. "That hole
doesn't look very wide."

"Come on, Happy," Max
said. "Stop being afraid."

But again Happy wished,
as he looked at the boat,
that it was back on the
beach, where he had
stayed.

Happy and Max approached the hole in the ship, and slowly they poked their heads inside.

"Don't be scared," Happy thought to himself. But he was still afraid, no matter how hard he tried.

"Agggggh!" barked Happy. "Max, whose eyes are those?"

"Agggggh!" yelled Max. "They belong to sea monsters, I suppose!"

"Sea monsters!" barked Happy, "Max, we should run!"

"Exploring the ocean was neat, but Max I've had enough fun."

The louder Happy and Max screamed, the more the sea monsters bubbled.

"Run Happy!" Max hollered.

"These sea monsters could mean trouble!"

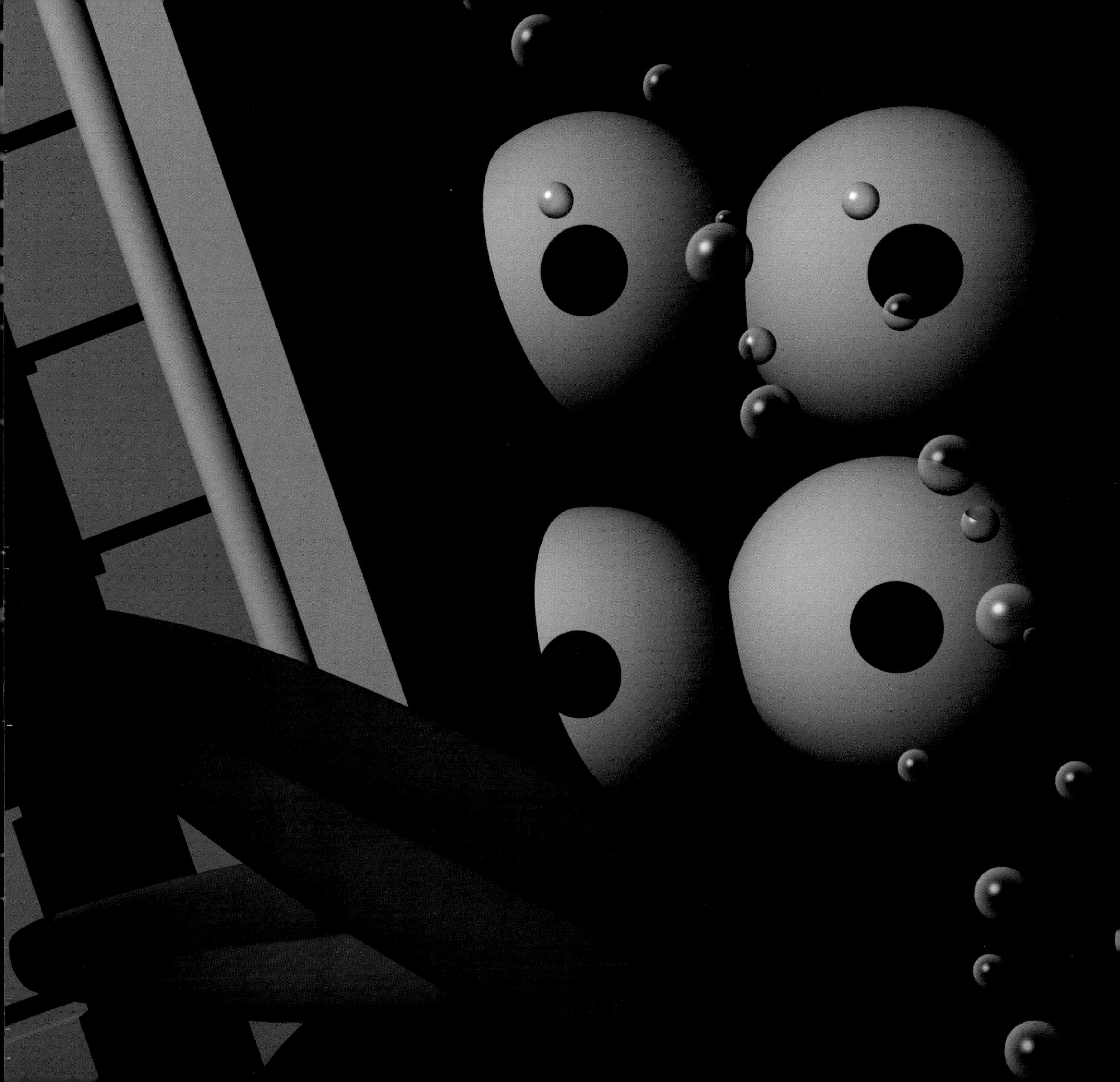

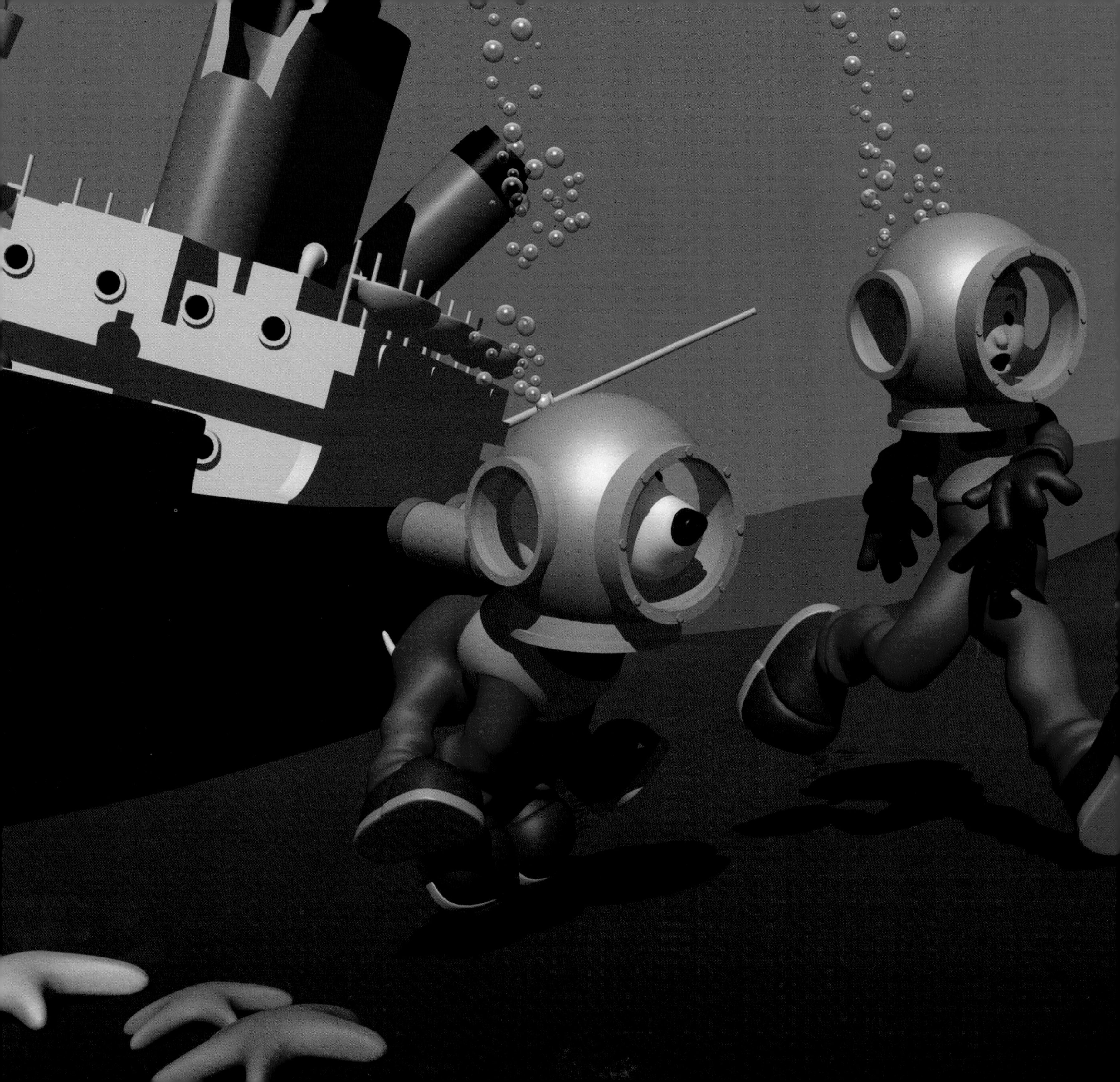

Happy and Max ran
from the ship, leaving
the monsters inside.

"Max let's find Trixie,"
Happy said. "She'll know
where we should hide!"

So Happy and Max made
their way back to the
shore, leaving the ship
for others to explore.

Back inside the ship, two fish had watched Happy and Max come and go.

"That was pretty funny," the first fish said. "That was quite a show!"

"Yeah," said the second fish, "everyday is the same. The sea divers run from the ship, saying that sea monsters are to blame."

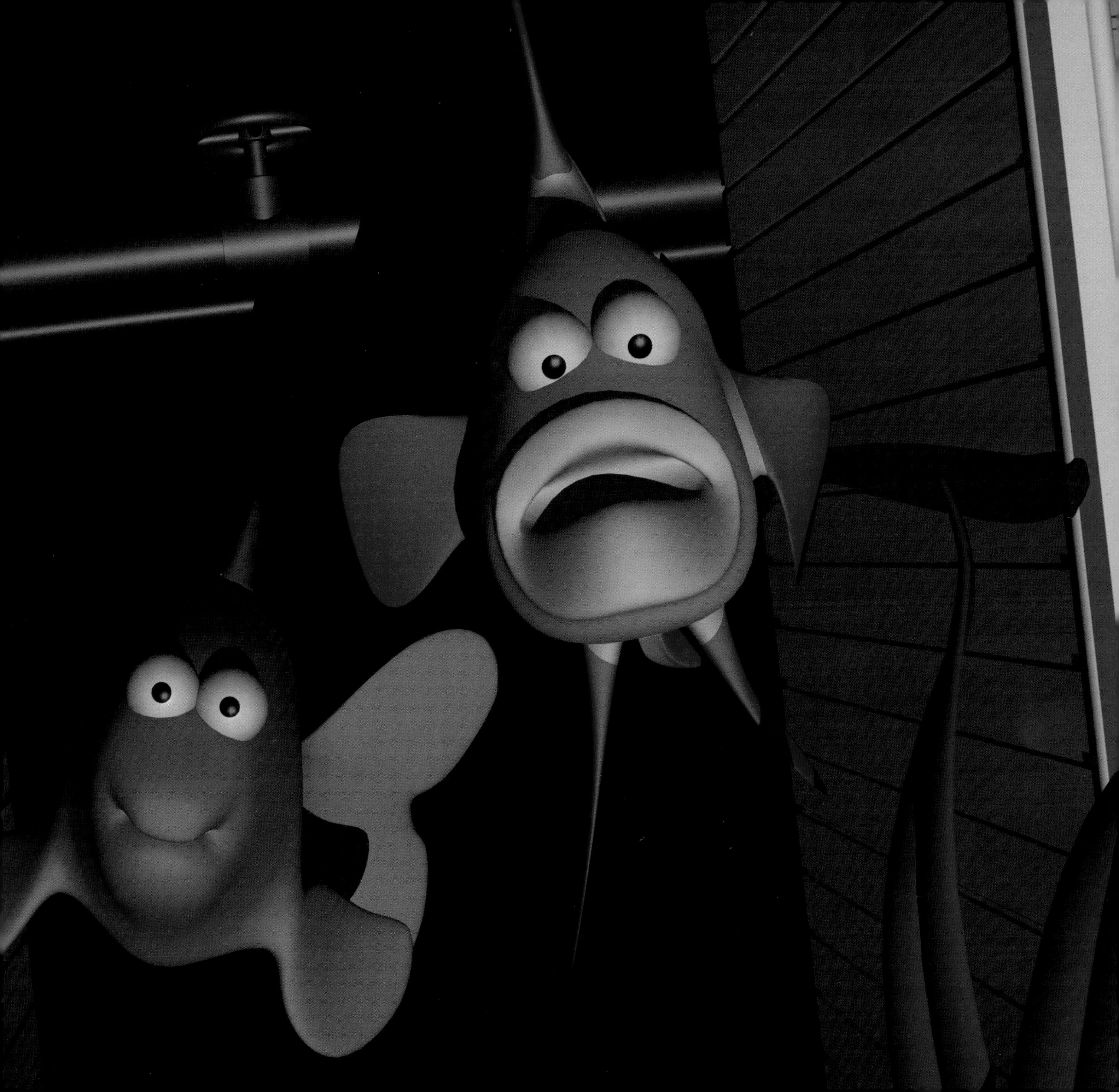

"I just don't get it," said the first fish. "What is it the sea divers fear?"

"There aren't any sea monsters inside this big ship, just this old antique mirror."

"The sea divers explore the ocean, and come across this ship along their way."

"But when they look in the mirror, their own reflection scares the sea divers away."

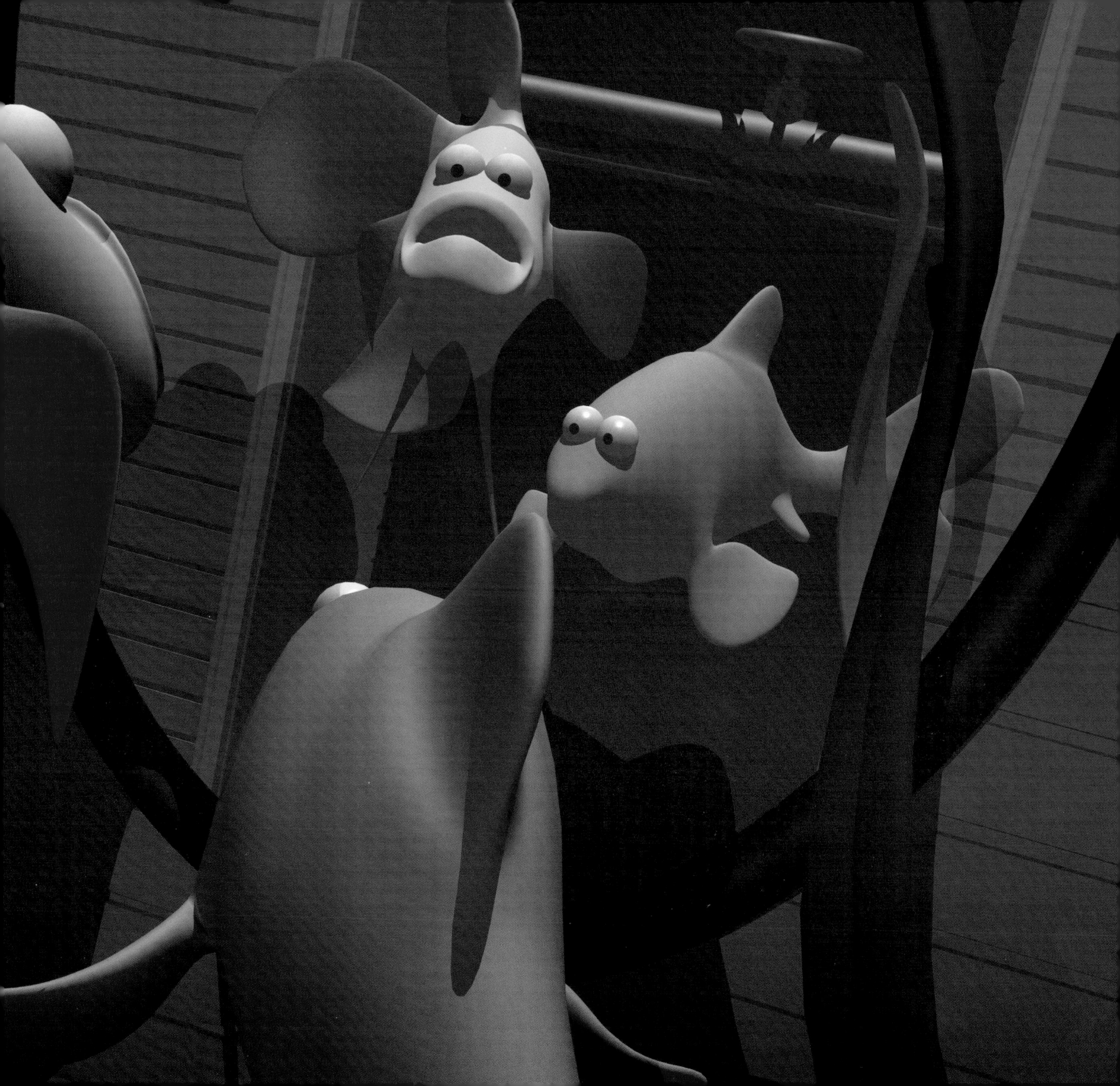

From the deep sea, Happy, Max, and Trixie made their way.

Back to the beach, on dry land, they could find other ways to play.

They had explored reefs and sunken ships, that they had found at the bottom of the sea.

But dry and on the beach, away from the sea monsters, is really where they wanted to be.

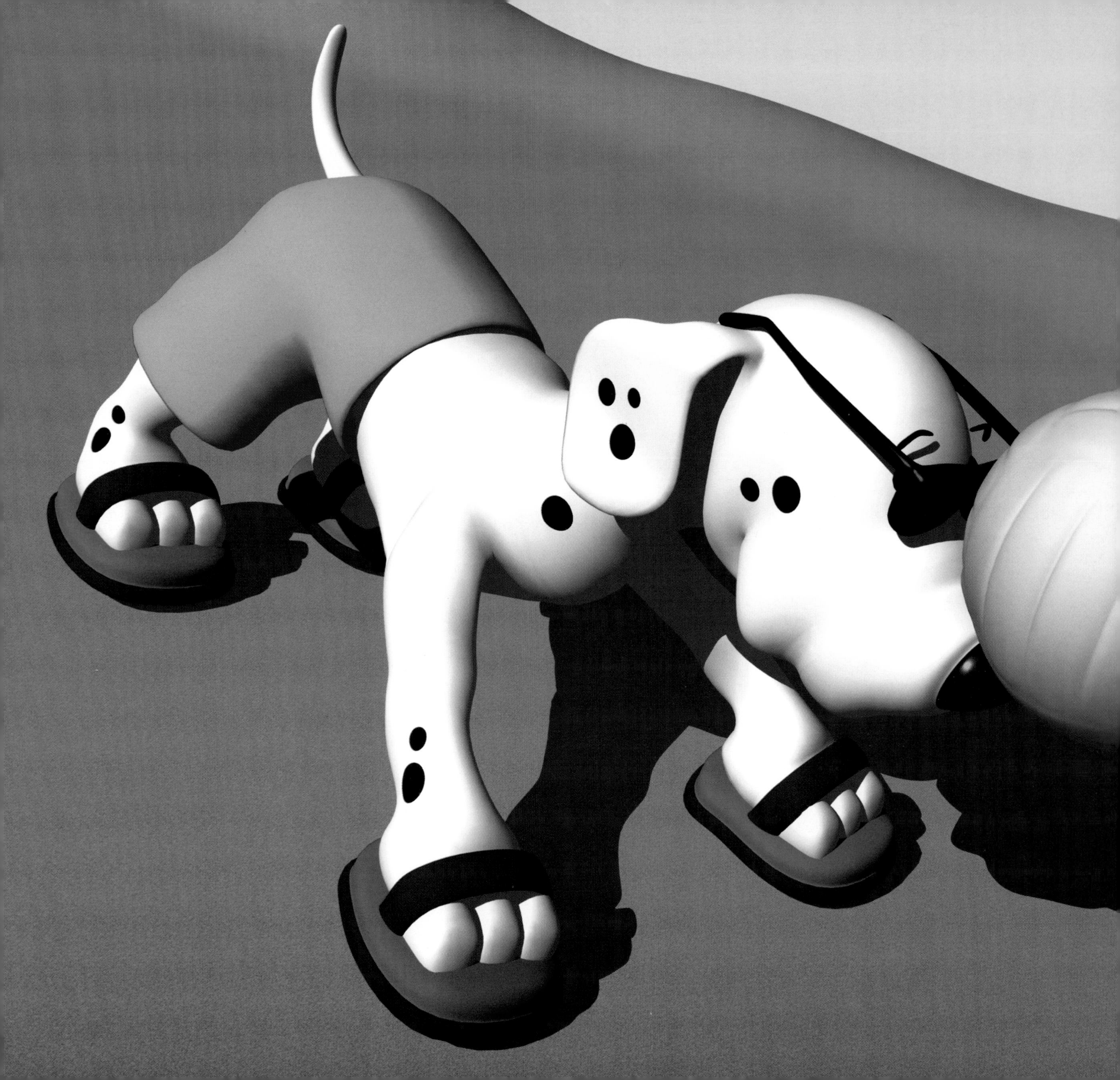

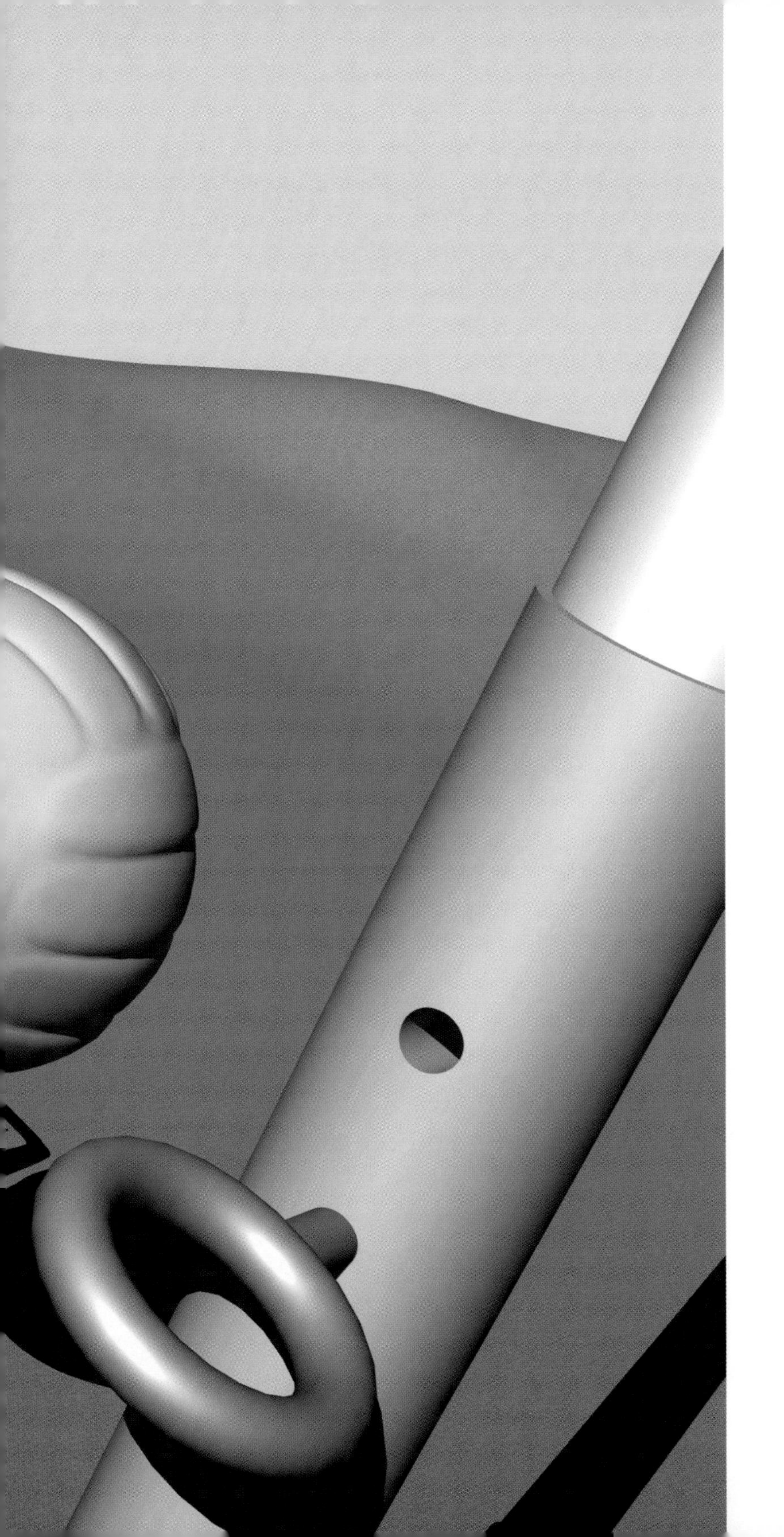

Happy and Max had their picnic lunch at the beach, where they had decided to stay.

"Come on Max," Happy barked, to his pal.

"I've got a volleyball, let's go play!"

Playing the Happy and Max Adventure Using Your Car Stereo or Audio-CD Player

To play the Happy and Max adventure using your car stereo or audio-CD player, simply insert the CD into your audio-CD player. Next, use your player's Seek button to advance to track 2 (the programs for your PC reside on track 1) and then press the Play button.

The audio CD assigns a track number to each page of the book. So, if you must stop and later restart the CD, you can use your player's Seek button to advance to the track where you left off.

Loading the Adventure Under Windows® 95 or Higher

Insert the Kids Interactive CD into your PC's CD-ROM drive. Your system, in turn, should automatically start the Happy and Max adventure program, displaying the program's main menu on your screen.

If your program does not start after you insert the CD, use your word processor or the Windows Notepad accessory to open the Readme file which resides on the CD-ROM. The Readme file will walk you through steps you can perform to run the program.

Loading the Adventure on a Mac

Insert the Kids Interactive CD into your Mac's CD-ROM drive. Your system, in turn, should display a CD-ROM icon on your desktop. Double click your mouse on the CD-ROM icon and open the Sunken folder. Within the folder, double click your mouse on the Sunken program icon to run the program.

Troubleshooting the Happy and Max CD-ROM

If you have trouble loading the Happy and Max adventure, use your word processor to open the Readme file which resides on the Happy and Max CD-ROM. The Readme file contains steps you can perform to run the program. In addition, you'll find more troubleshooting tips at the Happy and Max Web site at www.HappyAndMax.com.

Starting Your Adventure

After you load and run the Happy and Max adventure, your computer's screen will display the program's main menu as shown in Figure 1.

Figure 1 The Happy and Max main menu.

From within the main menu, you can start the interactive book, access the CD's two adventure games, or exit the program. In addition, the main menu provides an on-line help button, which will further explain how you can use the CD. To select an option within the main menu, click your mouse on the option's paw prints.

Reading Along with the Interactive CD

The Happy and Max CD-ROM contains an interactive version of the Happy and Max adventure. Within the interactive story, a narrator will read the story as the images appear on your computer screen. After the narrator stops reading the text, move your mouse within the image. When your mouse pointer changes from an arrow to a pointing hand, click your mouse button. You have found one of the story's interactive elements.

Depending on the element, your PC may show a close-up image of the object, play an audio file, or both. To resume the story, simply click your mouse a second time within the image.

To move from one page to the next within the story, click your mouse on the Next button. To move back to the previous page, click your mouse on the Back button.

Playing the Interactive Games

Each CD-ROM in the Happy and Max Adventure series includes two interactive computer games. To play the games, click your mouse on the main menu Play the Games option. The program, in turn, will display the Games Menu, as shown in Figure 2, from which you can choose the game you want to play.

Figure 2 The Happy and Max Games menu.

To play a game, click your mouse on the button that appears beneath the game you desire. The Happy and Max Sunken Ship Adventure includes a tic-tac-toe game and a submarine game with which you clean up the ocean by shooting the submarine's torpedoes at trash floating in the water.

How Do I Use the Interactive CD-ROM?

Ignore the CD and simply read the book

Each CD provides two interactive games

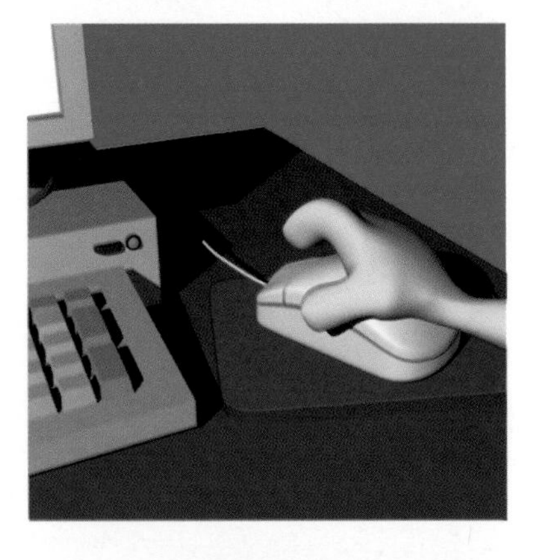

Interact with the story using a PC (running Windows 95 or higher) or a Mac

Put the CD in your stereo and listen while you read

Take the CD with you in the car and listen while you read